CAITLIN LONG

The shy girl and the sensitive guy (1)

Contents

1.

2.

3.

4.

5.

6.

7.

8.

9.

10.

11.

12.

13.

14.

15.

16.

17.

18.

19.

20.

Chapter 1

Emily Applebaum walked into Glennbrook High School with her head held high. She tossed her shoulder length brown hair and walked down the hallway to her locker.Emily looked at the posters for prom with her blue eyes. She hoped that she could find someone to take her to the dance when the time came. Emily couldn't wait to go to the homecoming game this weekend with her best friend Sam. Maybe she would finally find a guy who didn't find her weird. Emily got to her locker and took out her books. Sam ran up to her. She was a feisty blonde- haired green- eyed girl that loved to flirt with guys.

"Hi,Emily! Are you going to meet a guy at the homecoming game this weekend?" Sam asked.

"Sam, you know how I feel about meeting guys. Why should I even try to talk to them if I am just going to get rejected?" Emily responded.

Sam flipped her hair. "Girl, you seriously need to get laid! I can't believe that you're still a virgin!" Sam exclaimed. "Then again, it's not like you ever leave the house."

Emily shook her head and sighed. "You know how I feel about sex! I am not going to simply toss away my virginity. I'm saving myself for the right guy!"

Sam sighed wearily. "Emily... at this rate, you'll be thirty years old before you get laid!"

"That is not true!" argued Emily.

Sam lays on the sarcasm. "Really, Emily?"

Emily, clearly annoyed said"Yes, really, Samantha."

Sam glared at Emily as though she spit in her coffee. Emily knew how much Sam didn't like it when she said her full name.

Sam huffed angrily."You don't need to bring my full name into this Emily".

Emily was apologetic and held her hands anxiously. "I'm sorry Sam. I just don't like it when you push me."

Sam tried to cheer Emily up."Why don't you talk to a guy at the game?"

Emily hesitantly says"I'm scared, Sam. What if he is not interested?"

Sam enthusiastically replied."You never know if you don't try, Emily".

Emily realized that Sam was right. She had to put herself out there. Sam and Emily made their way to history class. Emily wondered if she was going to meet the right guy at the homecoming game. Or if she would just stammer her way into a dismissal from a cute boy.

Elijah Henderson was the type of guy that always wanted to know how his friends were doing and if they needed any advice from him on homework or girls. He was a brown-haired and brown- eyed guy that liked to play video games and jam on his guitar. Elijah had three friends. John Carpenter who was a brown- haired brown eyed guy who liked to be serious. Jason Walker was a red-haired,green-eyed guy who was into writing short stories. Samuel Parks was a black-haired guy with one blue eye and one green eye. He was known for always cracking a joke, especially one that was dirty.

Elijah was walking in the hallway with John, Jason and Samuel.John started talking about the homecoming game.

"Elijah, man, you need to find yourself a girl".

Elijah started getting annoyed.

Elijah sighed."John, I have told you before. No girl is going to be attracted to me. I'm too much of a nerd for girls at this school".

Samuel added." Dude, you need to sixty- nine a girl so bad, that your dick comes out with so much semen. That your juices get all over the girl and she comes so hard that she squirts on you."

Elijah was shocked by this and said." Whoa, Samuel, that is way too much information dude. You know that I haven't had sex in two years. Not since Becca fucking cheated on me. ''

Samuel was empathic to Elijah and put his arm around him. "Elijah, look, you need to get over that bitch. She was not good for you. Plus, you never know. You could meet a nice girl who actually treats you right".

Elijah was doubtful of this."How would I know, though?"

Samuel added. "Trust me, dude, you will know".

Jason chimed in. "Elijah, Samuel may be onto something. You need to at least try to talk to girls at the game".

Elijah was hesitant but he agreed."Okay, fine, I will talk to girls at the game this weekend if it means that you guys will get off my back". Samuel, John and Jason answered in unison. "That is all we ask Elijah." Elijah was worried that any girl that he will talk to this weekend will laugh in his face, but he made a promise to his friends.

3

If he backed out, his friends would be upset. Maybe Samuel was right. He could probably find a nice girl that actually laughed at his jokes. He would have to wait until the weekend to find out if there was a girl who actually saw the real him.

Chapter 2

Emily was excited for the homecoming game tonight. She was also an anxious mess worrying about what boys would say to her when she talked to them. She was getting ready for the night with Sam. Sam helped her realize that she could find a guy that gave her butterflies and holds her hand when she is scared. Emily took deep breaths and sang her favorite song "Breathe (2AM)" by Anna Nalick. She started to calm down and Sam looked at her with so much pride.

"I'm telling you Emily you will find that special someone tonight that you have always been talking about."

Emily is glad that Sam is happy for her and claps her hands." Thanks so much for helping me pick out an outfit, Sam."

Sam twists her hips. "No problem my little candy cane."

Emily has a look of surprise on her face."I can't believe that you remember that nickname Sam."

Sam has an expectant look on her face."Well Emily you do love candy canes a lot."

Emily smiles and points at herself and then Sam. "Yes I do and you love Bam Margera a lot also Sam."

Sam admits. "That is so true Emily. We both have our addictions. You are addicted to candy, and I am addicted to a hot man. That I can never have unfortunately."

Emily puts her knuckles near her eyes and pretends to cry. "Oh boo hoo Sam. You could get any guy you want. Whereas I have to try to talk to guys in order for them to notice me."

Sam has a patronizing look on her face." Oh come on Emily you just need to be more confident."

''Now are you ready to go girl?'' Sam asked.

Emily has a confident smirk on her face."Yes I am Sam. Let's go find some dudes."

Sam beams with a smile from ear to ear." I am so proud of you right now Em, like you have no idea."

Emily has her hands to her sides and looks at Sam "You are helping me feel better Sam. Thank you for making me see that I am beautiful especially with this makeover."

Sam puts her arms around Emily affectionately." I told you that you didn't need to get that dolled up. You just needed to have your hair curled and put on a little bit of lip gloss."

Emily says with a grin " I still appreciate it though Sam."

Sam and Emily hugged.

Sam adds,"Your welcome Emily. Now as you said let's go find some dudes."

Emily laughed.

Emily chimes in."Yes Sam let's go to the game and talk to guys." Emily was wearing a blue blouse with jean shorts. While Sam was wearing a black leather jacket with a green t shirt and black pants. Sam and Emily left for the game each wondering if they were going to get any numbers from guys.

Elijah was getting ready for the game at his house with John, Jason and Samuel giving him tips for talking to girls. John gestures with his hands."Make sure to ask for her number dude."

Jason chimes in."Make sure to hold her hand and make sure that she is okay if you are taking her to a scary movie." Samuel adds."Make sure to fuck her so hard that she screams your name really loud."

Elijah screams."Okay I get it, you guys want me to have a girlfriend."

John pleads. " We are just trying to help you out Elijah."

Samuel declares. "Yeah and if that means that you get to lick her pussy. I say go for it man."

Elijah is exasperated."You and your dirty talk Samuel.

"What if a girl doesn't want me to lick her pussy?'' Elijah asked.

Samuel chimes in. "You never know if you don't ask."

Elijah annoyingly heaves." I am not going to ask a girl that on her first date Samuel. I am just going to talk to her and see what she likes."

Samuel adds."Okay whatever floats your boat man"

Jason chimes in. "I think that Elijah is right Samuel. He needs to talk to girls first."

Elijah has a big smile on his face."Thanks Jason."

Jason smiles as well. "You are welcome Elijah".

Jason and Elijah hugged it out.

Samuel called out."Okay guys, let's go bang some chicks."

Elijah and Jason just rolled their eyes at Samuel. He was the dirtiest thinking person that they have ever met.

John chimed in. "Let's go have some fun guys." Making Jason and Elijah feel better about being around Samuel when he gets horny. Elijah left for the homecoming game with John and Jason, while Samuel trailed behind making dirty jokes on the way to the car.

Sam and Emily made it to the homecoming game and found their seats in the bleachers.

Sam shouted. "This is going to be so much fun Emily".

Emily smiled as bright as the sun. "I'm actually excited for this Sam".

Sam has a look of excitement on her face. "I'm glad that you are going to talk to a guy Em. Who knows, maybe he will like the same kind of music that you do".

Emily replies with a grin. "I can only hope that I can be that lucky Sam".

The two of them cheered on the Glennbrook Gators as they were playing the Hodgson Hornets in the most important game of the season. When halftime came around, Emily went to the refreshment stand to get a pretzel. Sam noticed some guys near the stand and eyed them up and down while biting her lip slightly. "See you in a little bit Em. I have some nice prospects I need to investigate". ''Hi boys!'' She said sensually rubbing the arm of each guy.

Emily thought to herself, *if only I could talk to guys that confidently*. Emily made her way to get a pretzel and as she was walking, she bumped into someone. She looked up into the most beautiful brown eyes that she had ever seen. Suddenly there was a cute guy in front of her. She tried to think of something to say.

All she could think of was

''Hhhhhi''.

Emily wondered. *I really hope this guy doesn't think I'm a creep.*

Elijah was just going to grab a hot dog when this cute girl bumped into him. She stammered with her words but he just thought *wow she is so adorable*. He decided to help her out."Hi. I'm Elijah. I think we accidentally bumped into each other. It's nice to meet you though". She looked shocked that he actually spoke to her. She started talking though.

"I'm Emily. You are really cute. I can't believe that I just said that. I don't really talk to guys that much and I should just stop talking".

Elijah thought. *wow she is really honest and cute.*

He reassured her."No no you don't have to do that."

"I don't?'' Emily asked.

Elijah puts her mind at ease."Yeah you don't. Emily is a pretty name by the way."

He could see her cheeks blush and he wondered if a guy had ever complimented her before.

Emily smiled."Thank you Elijah. You are really sweet".

The way she said his name did something to his penis. He hadn't been attracted to a girl since Becca and this was instant. His cock immediately got hard when she said his name. He had to rein in the lust so he didn't scare her away. She seemed the type to be inexperienced sexually and he wanted to give her pleasure when she was ready.

Elijah gestured with his hands."Your welcome Emily. Could I maybe get your number so we can go out?"

He saw Emily get a surprised look on her face and he realized that a guy had never asked for her number before.

Elijah thought. *She is so beautiful and yet she is single. Are guys just idiots?*

Whatever the case, he was glad that she didn't have a boyfriend. She was a nice girl. He would just need to take things slow with her. Start with kissing and then work up to fucking. All in due time. He wouldn't force her to do anything she didn't want to.

He finally heard her say

"Sure".

He took out his phone and they exchanged numbers.

Emily handed Elijah back his phone. "Thanks Emily. Are you free tomorrow?''

Emily got her phone back from Elijah."Your welcome Elijah and yes".

He wanted to hear her say yes to more things in the future.

Elijah held out his hand to Emily." Good. Can I hold your hand and walk you back to your seat?''

Emily has a surprised look on her face." I wanted to get a pretzel. Wait did you just say that you want to hold my hand? That is so cute.
"

Elijah shrugged. "Yeah. I didn't know if you would like that or not. Most girls would find that weird".

Emily beamed." I'm not like most girls and I have the feeling that you aren't like most guys."

Elijah smiled."You would be correct Emily. I can get you a pretzel by the way".

Emily waved her hand to the side."You don't have to Elijah."

Elijah smirked." I know I don't have to but I want to Emily".

Emily put her hand on her chest."Wow. You are a gentleman. I have always liked gentlemen".

Elijah bowed to her on his knees." I aim to please Emily".

Emily put her hand in his."And please you shall Elijah".

Elijah kissed her hand and stood up."Let's get a pretzel then and a hot dog Emily."

Emily smirked."Sounds good Elijah".

He reached out to hold her hand and saw her smile.

Elijah pondered. *Wow she has a great smile. Her hands are really warm. She must be a great person.*

He held her hand from the refreshment stand all the way back to her seat.

He thought. *How lucky am I to find such a nice girl.*

Emily couldn't believe that she met such a nice guy.

She thought. *The fact that he is cute just makes it even better. It also doesn't hurt that he asked me out.*

Sam came up to Emily noticing her smile.

Sam grinned."Em you finally met a guy. I can tell by the look on your face. Good for you."

Emily couldn't stop smiling." Thanks Sam. He is actually really nice. Plus he asked for my number."

Sam patted Emily on the shoulder." Go Em. He must really like you. What's his name?''

Emily beamed."His name is Elijah. He held my hand.''

Sam has a shocked expression on her face."Wow you actually found a guy that could be from one of the books that you read. I'm happy for you Em.''

Emily moved her head to the side feeling bashful all of a sudden."I'm happy too Sam. Let's watch the rest of the game."

Sam pouted."Oh you are no fun Em. Let's talk about Elijah. How big do you think his penis is?''

Emily is annoyed."Oh Sam, I didn't look at his penis".

Sam is very curious."Why not Em?''

Emily is flippant."Sam, I don't think about a guy's penis".

Sam looks at Emily with sarcasm."Oh Emily you need to do something for yourself. Tickle the pickle, so to speak."

Emily is confused."I don't even know how to do that.''

Sam puts her hand against her forehead."Oh Em you haven't ever masturbated?''

Emily gives Sam the death glare."No I haven't Sam. Can you please keep it down?"

Sam placed her finger on her chin and started to think."Okay. I know what we need to do. We need to get you a vibrator."

Emily is hesitant."Where would we get a vibrator Sam?''

Sam looks at Emily with a shit eating grin on her face."Trust me Em. I know places.''

Sam dragged Emily away from the bleachers and towards a sex shop for the vibrator.

Emily is baffled."How will I know how to use one of these things Sam?''

Sam puts her arm around Emily."Oh trust me Em you will know".

After buying the vibrator, Emily went home to try out the sex toy. Emily walked into her bedroom, sat on the bed and pulled down her pants. She then pulled down her underwear and put the vibrator near her vagina.

When they were at the store Sam took her to the side and said ''make sure to place it close to your clit Em. That's where all the magic happens''.

Remembering that piece of information, Emily tried to find her clit which took 20 minutes. She felt like she had to find the needle in the vaginal haystack. Finally she felt this interesting sensation which traveled all over her body. She thought of Elijah and the feelings became more intense. She screamed in pleasure while rubbing the vibrator all over her clit in a circular motion.

Emily screams.''Yessssss Elijah.''

Her cries could be heard throughout the room.

Her whole body tingled by the time she was done.

She thought. *Wow now I know why people have sex. That was fucking amazing. Sam was right. Masturbating is fun.*

Elijah went back to his seat at the game.

John smiled. "Elijah you look happy dude."

Samuel chimed in."He must have fucked a girl".

Jason shook his finger at Samuel. "Samuel we must not assume that he had sexual relations with a girl just because he is smiling."

Elijah waved his hand in the air as a white flag of sorts. "I met someone. She is amazing and sweet."

John, Jason and Samuel interrupted in agreement."Wow Elijah actually met a nice girl."

Elijah sighed. "I'm serious dudes, I think she is the one. Her name is Emily, and she is so beautiful".

John nodded his head. "We are so happy for you Elijah".

Jason smiled. "Yes Elijah you have come a long way from your past. You have been hurt before but you have not let that stop you from finding love."

Elijah turned toward Jason. "Thanks Jason.''

Jason pivoted toward Elijah. "You are welcome young Elijah".

Samuel interjected. "You definitely need to work your way up to fucking her though man."

Elijah threw his head back in laughter. "I know Samuel and I will. I'm taking baby steps."

Samuel patted Elijah on the back. "That's great man. I am so proud of you for finding someone."

Elijah smiled. "Thanks Samuel."

Samuel put his arm around Elijah. "You're welcome Elijah."

The four friends had a big group hug. After the hug they watched the football game and talked about boobs.

After the game, Elijah got home and thought about Emily. He couldn't wait to see her again. He would text her tomorrow to figure out when they could go on their first date. He will make the occasion romantic for her. He had a feeling that she was into romance movies. In fact, most girls were into sappy romance movies like The Notebook. If she wanted roses he would give her roses. She made him want to be a better man. He wanted to treat her like a queen and shower her with kisses. Just thinking of her turned him on so much that he had to jerk off. He went into his bedroom, tore off his pants and underwear. He laid in bed and played with his penis. He thought of Emily and her giving him a blow job. He started to get a familiar feeling in his cock. He continued to jerk his penis, working it until his semen sprayed out all over his stomach. He screamed in pleasure. "EMMMILLLY!!!" He felt rejuvenated after cuming and realized that he hadn't cum that hard in a really long time. Emily was special and maybe just maybe she might be his soulmate. Elijah thought. *Normally I don't believe in that kind of thing but everything happens for a reason. I think I might fall for this girl.*

Chapter 3

The next morning

Emily woke up with a big smile on her face. She couldn't wait to go out with Elijah. Emily wondered.*What shall I wear today? I want to look cute.* She got out of bed and went to her closet. Emily looked through her wardrobe to find an outfit. She picked out a pink t-shirt and blue jeans. As Emily was getting dressed, she got a text on her phone. She went to check who it was and smiled. Elijah had messaged her.

"Hi Emily. It's Elijah. I already miss you. What time do you want to go out?"

Emily texted back. "Hi Elijah. We can go out at 6 and get dinner. I miss you too. " They exchanged texts back and forth. Elijah texted. "Great. 6 works for me and dinner would be awesome. What are you going to do until then?" Emily shot back." I'm probably going to read some romance books and listen to music. `` After she texted that, she thought. *Wow does he think I'm some wierd girl who reads books at candlelight?* He texted back." Wow you read. That's awesome. I'm not really into books but you must be really smart".

Emily fired back."Thank you. I have always loved books. My mom used to read to me when I was little. What are you going to do?"

Emily changed into her clothes.

Elijah flung back." Probably going to play the guitar and listen to some music."

Emily replied. "You play the guitar? That's so cool."

She always wanted a guy that played the guitar. Her vagina instantly got wet just thinking about him playing the guitar.

Elijah wrote back. "Thanks. I started playing a few years ago. Do you play any instruments?''

Emily answered. "I don't play any instruments but I sing".

Elijah replied. "That's great. Could I maybe hear you sometime?"

Emily responded. "Maybe. I get nervous when I sing in front of people."

Elijah texted back. "It will just be me. If it will help I could play a song on the guitar and you could sing".

Emily acknowledged."That sounds like fun".

Elijah sent back. "Maybe that could be our second date".

Emily returned with "maybe".

Just then Elijah started calling her.

Emily answered.

"Hello".

Elijah reciprocated."Hi. I just wanted to hear your voice."

Emily smiled." Aww that's so sweet. I like hearing your voice."

Elijah said. "Really? I like hearing your voice too".

Emily sat on the bed looking at her nails. "That's good."

Elijah responded. "Yeah". I want to say something and I don't want to scare you away".

Emily has a curious look on her face. "What is it?''

17

Elijah commented. "I'm really attracted to you more than I have ever been to a girl".

Emily is surprised. "Really? You are attracted to me?''

Elijah retorted. "Don't sound so surprised Emily. You are so damn beautiful''.

Emily twirled her hair around her fingers." Thank you Elijah. No guy has ever called me beautiful before".

Elijah responded. "That is a shame Emily. You are the most beautiful girl in the world. The fact that no guy taught you that is an injustice that must be rectified."

Emily sat up in bed."How?''

Elijah countered. "By me showing you how beautiful you are tonight. First dinner and then a night under the stars which will be romantic".

Emily grinned. "How did you know that I like looking at the stars?''

Elijah replied. "I didn't. I just figured that you liked romance books which means that you like romance movies. I want to make this date special for you because I already feel like you are special to me".

Emily looked at her nails again."That is the most romantic thing that a guy has ever said to me".

Elijah responded. "Good. I'm glad. I'm going to take things slow with you because I don't want to rush things. You let me know when you are ready for sex. If that is several months or a year from now I will wait."

Emily replied." I honestly haven't had sex. Until recently I didn't even know how to masturbate".

She thought. *Why did I just say that? Guys don't want to hear about that.* Elijah broke her thoughts.

Elijah was surprised. "Really? You didn't ever touch down there when you were younger."

Emily explained. "No. I didn't know how. They don't teach you that kind of thing in health class".

Elijah was very understanding. "Yeah. That is true. You have to experiment with that on your own. I won't ask you what you used if you don't want me to. I won't ask who you thought of either".

Emily quickly said. "It was you". *Emily just stop fucking talking. Now he probably thinks you are some creep.*

Elijah remarked. "What were we doing?"

Emily got nervous. "I-I-I don't remember."

Elijah retorted. "I don't know if I should say this, but in mine you were giving me a blow job".

Emily was curious. "I don't even know how to do that".

Elijah was compassionate." I could teach you eventually. I honestly didn't think that you would bring up masturbation. It just makes me want to fu- be with you even more. Sorry about that. I probably shouldn't say fuck to you. Honestly you deserve better than that. You deserve to be worshipped and adored".

Emily beamed. "Wow. You are amazing."

She could hear Elijah laugh.

Elijah replied. "You don't think I'm weird or creepy? Most girls think that I'm this eccentric nerd that plays a lot of video games."

Emily smirked. "I told you. I'm not like most girls, plus I'm a nerd".

Elijah responded. "You are? Wow you are the hottest nerd that I have ever met."

Emily laughed. "Thank you."

Elijah answered. "Your welcome".

Emily was hesitant. "Maybe I should wait to ask this in person."

Elijah was curious. "What is it?''

Emily blurted out. " I wanted to ask how many girls you have had sex with?''

Elijah thought. *Wow I only met this girl yesterday and she has the balls to ask me how many girls I have slept with. She is so sassy and I love it. The fact that she was thinking about me when she came is so fucking hot that I want to cum right now. The thing is I don't know how she would react to me cuming on the phone. I'd better save it for after the phone call. I'm going to be honest with her. She has been honest with me about everything. She is not Becca. Emily is better than Becca. She's smart, sweet, kind and funny. I could talk to her on the phone every day. Shit she's waiting for me to say something. Don't say anything dirty Elijah. Though she said plenty earlier. One day I want to see her masturbate and I want both of us to cum together in unison. I'd better say something now.*

Elijah smiled. "I have had sex with two girls. I thought that I was in love with them but I wasn't".

Emily replied. "Wow. That's great."

Elijah has a look of shock on his face. "It is? You really don't respond like a typical girl".

Emily retorted. "True."

Elijah sat on his bed with a big grin on his face. "I like that though. Shit, I just realized that I have to meet up with my friends. Every Saturday we eat pizza and watch king of the hill."

Emily acknowledged. "That sounds like fun. Are you going to play your guitar?''

Elijah thought. *Wow she remembered that I play the guitar. That's awesome.*

Elijah smirked."Yes I will play my guitar for a little bit before they come over. I will see you at 6 Emily."

Emily replied."Sounds good Elijah. I will see you at 6 then."

Elijah touched his hair. "Bye Emily."

Emily responded. "Bye Elijah."

As he hung up the phone, his penis was rock hard.

"Aw shit. This girl has got me good."

He whipped out his cock and proceeded to cum. Elijah came so hard that he got jizz all over his legs. He quickly grabbed a towel and scrubbed the semen off his legs. Elijah changed his clothes and grabbed his guitar. He played "Stairway to Heaven" by Led Zeppelin. Twenty minutes later, John, Samuel and Jason showed up with pizza.

John had the pizza box in his hand. "We brought pizza."

Samuel chimed in. " We also brought some porn just in case we get horny."

Jason interrupted. "Oh Samuel. We will not be watching porn at this time."

Elijah gave his friends high fives. "You guys. I have my first date with Emily tonight."

Samuel interjected. "Aww shit. Elijah is going to have sex tonight."

Elijah rolled his eyes. "Samuel. I told you that I'm going to wait to have sex with Emily. I don't want to freak her out. Surprisingly she didn't care that I only had sex with two girls."

Jason smiled. "That is great dear Elijah. I have a feeling that Emily is going to make you very happy."

Elijah fist bumped with Jason. "Thanks Jason."

Jason fist bumped him back. "Your welcome Elijah."

Samuel recited. "Okay let's watch king of the hill."

Elijah put a hand over his forehead in relief. "Finally Samuel says something that is not dirty."

John puts his hands palms up and shrugs his shoulders. "It was bound to happen eventually."

All four guys laughed in unison and sat down to watch king of the   hill.

Chapter 4

Emily felt great after talking to Elijah on the phone. She started to get this tingle in her breasts. Emily hadn't felt this way before. She realized that she was horny. Emily knew what she had to do. She had to use the vibrator. Emily took off her clothes, laid in bed and grabbed the vibrator. She then started to flick her bean and touch her breasts all the while her orgasms got more intense. Emily pictured her and Elijah having sex in her head with her being on top. She had her biggest orgasm ever, her body pulsing all over. Emily yelled."Elijaaaaaaaaaaaaaaaaaaaaaaaaaah!'' Her vagina tingled after she came. She felt amazing. Emily changed into a blue shirt and blue jeans. She read her favorite book "Sundays at Tiffany's" by James Patterson until she went on her date with Elijah.

Elijah got ready for his date with Emily. He put on his red shirt and black pants. Elijah combed his hair. He put on his socks and shoes. Elijah went out the door. He called Emily.

" Hi. Do you want to meet up at the restaurant or do you want me to pick you up?" He heard Emily say. "Hi. You can pick me up. I'm at 541 Hillside Road." Elijah started getting his coat on and answered, "thanks Emily. I will see you in a few." He felt Emily's anticipation through the phone."Your welcome Elijah."

He went to his car and drove to Emily's house. Elijah made it to her house and got out of the car. He walked to the door and rang the doorbell. Elijah heard the door open and saw Emily. He thought. *She looks amazing.*

Elijah smiled. "Hi Emily. You look beautiful."

Emily beamed back."Hi Elijah. Thank you."

Elijah thought. *Wow she is really cute.*

Elijah fixed his hair. "Your welcome Emily. Shall we?''

He put his arm out gesturing to Emily.

Emily smirked."We shall kind sir."

Emily put her arm through his and they walked to his car.

He liked having her arm through his arm. Elijah felt it was natural for her arm to be there. He enjoyed walking her to his car. Elijah opened the car door for her and Emily had a shocked look on her face.

He wondered. *She must not be used to guys holding the door for her. I am definitely going to treat her right.* Emily got in the passenger seat and Elijah closed the door. He went to the driver's side, opened the door and got in the driver's seat closing the door.

Elijah put his seatbelt on and turned to Emily.

"I'm glad that we are doing this."

Emily looked at him. "Me too Elijah. I really like you."

She smiled at him and it went right to his cock.

Elijah grinned back at her."I really like you too."

He leaned in and kissed Emily. She kissed him back and his penis was rock hard. After 5 minutes, they stopped kissing.

Elijah felt embarrassed. "I'm sorry that I kissed you so quickly. I normally don't kiss on the first date but you are special". Emily smiled again.

"Thanks Elijah. This may seem awkward but that was my first kiss."

He wasn't surprised that she hadn't been kissed before.

Elijah was curious. "Did you like it?''

Emily played with her hands. "I liked it a lot. You are a really good kisser."

Elijah was very pleased by the compliment."Thanks Emily. You are a good kisser too."

Emily looks surprised."Really?''

Elijah nods his head. "Really."

He thought. *Emily is so different from other girls. She is sweet and honest while also being funny. For that being her first kiss she sure put a lot of passion into that kiss. I can't wait to have dinner with her and look at the stars.*

Emily couldn't stop smiling. Elijah was so adorable. She couldn't believe that he opened the car door for her. Emily felt like she was on cloud nine. They made it to Olive Garden. Elijah opened the door for Emily again.

Emily smiled. "Thank you Elijah."

Elijah held her hand."Your welcome Em."

Emily has a look of shock on her face. "Em? My best friend Sam calls me that".

Elijah pouted. "You don't like it?"

Emily has a straight face and then smirks. "No. I mean I do like it."

Elijah smiles. "Good. Let's eat dinner."

Emily agreed."Yes, let's eat."

They walked into the restaurant, found a table and Elijah pulled out a chair for Emily.

Emily is surprised."You are seriously so sweet."

Elijah grins. "I try."

Emily smiles."You succeed."

They both sat in their chairs. When the waiter came, they ordered their food. Elijah and Emily talked about their likes, dislikes. They found out that they have a lot in common.

Emily asked. "What's your favorite food?"

Elijah blurted out."Burritos."

Emily held his hand from across the table. "Awesome. I love mexican food."

Elijah kept looking at her."Cool. I love pickles."

Emily had a sour expression on her face.''I don't like pickles, but that's fine that you do."

Elijah massaged her hands. "Thanks. I don't like mayonnaise."

Emily was honest."I like mayonnaise with tuna. That's okay, that you don't like it."

Elijah was curious. "What's your favorite thing to do?"

Emily answered. "I love reading, baking and minigolf."

Elijah smiled."I love minigolf too. We should do minigolf one day."

Emily looked into his warm brown eyes. "Sounds good Elijah."

She thought. *He is definitely the one. Elijah is the guy that I have been waiting for.*

Elijah was having so much fun talking to Emily and eating dinner with her. He paid for the dinner and saw that Emily was smiling. Elijah was glad that he made her happy. He wanted to continue to make her happy. Elijah got up, pulled out Emily's chair and helped her out of the chair.

Emily was still grinning."Thank you."

Elijah took her hand. "Your welcome Emily".

They went to Elijah's car and drove to the park.

Elijah replied. "I really enjoy spending time with you."

Emily was keeping her hands in her lap."I enjoy spending time with you too."

Elijah kept both hands on the steering wheel. " Before I take you home, I want to take you to a park. We can watch the stars."

Emily wanted to cry happy tears. "Elijah, you are so romantic."

Elijah smiled."I try Emily, I try."

Elijah and Emily made it to the park and got out of the car. They sat on the grass next to each other while looking at the stars.

Emily looked at the stars.''This is so beautiful."

Elijah looked at Emily."Yes it is."

He could see her cheeks flush.

Elijah thought. *Wow. She is so fucking adorable. I love the way her cheeks turn pink when she is embarrassed. This is such a cute quirk.*

He leaned in to kiss her. She kissed him right back with fervor. They continued to kiss for 10 mins and then he put his arm around Emily. He could get used to laying here with her. Elijah kept looking at Emily in awe of her.

He thought. *I can't believe that I am with the most beautiful girl that I have ever met and she is so sweet.*

They sat there on the grass for what seemed like hours just staring at the stars. Elijah was in shock that he and Emily could sit without saying a word to each other. He felt so comfortable with Emily more than he had with his ex girlfriends. She was so different from anyone that he had seen before. This was a good thing though because he had been with girls that didn't care about him; they just wanted someone to take advantage of. Finally Emily broke the silence.

"I haven't had sex. I mean I have read romance novels where there were sex scenes in it but I havent done anything with any guys".

Elijah brought his attention to Emily and he wasn't surprised that she hadn't had sex before. She seemed very innocent to him like she hadn't even given a blowjob before. He actually liked that she was being honest and that she hadn't done anything sexual before. Elijah wanted to show Emily how to have sex and give blowjobs gradually. Elijah didn't want another guy teaching her how to give herself pleasure or how to please him because that guy wouldn't care about her needs. He desired to please her and make her moan so hard that she tingles all over her body. Elijah needed to remind himself that he couldn't do that just yet even as his cock got hard.

Elijah looked at Emily. "That's great."

Emily was confused. "It is? You don't think it's weird?"

Elijah grinned. "No. Why would I think that it's weird?"

Emily looked down at the grass. "Because most girls would have had sex by now".

Elijah gently used his hand on her chin to get Emily to look at him again. " I'm pretty sure you are not like most girls which is why I like you. It is also why I am holding myself back from fucking you right now. Normally I don't kiss on the first date but I wanted to kiss you. I also wouldn't care about going too fast with other girls but with you it's different. You are a delicate flower Emily that I want to cherish   and   keep   safe   and   pleasure."

Chapter 5

Emily couldn't believe what Elijah had just said. He wanted to have sex with her? No guy had ever wanted to have sex with her before let alone look in her direction. The thing that he said about her being a flower was just about the sweetest thing that any boy has ever said to her. Elijah wanted to protect her and Emily realized that she wanted a guy to be there for her. Fuck society for telling her to be an independent woman who doesn't need a guy to be happy. Emily understood that the right guy can make a girl feel like she can do anything she sets her mind to. Being with Elijah has given her the chance to be the best version of herself.

Emily is surprised. " I did not expect you to say that. I was hoping that you liked me because I like you too."

She could see a big smile on Elijah's face when she said that.

Elijah continued to hold her hand."I guessed that you liked me by the way that you were kissing me. I want to ask you something but I don't want to go too fast with you."

Emily was curious. "What is it?''

Elijah looked at her."We can kiss in other places; that is if you want to".

Emily was confused."Other places? Wait do you mean-"

Elijah interrupted. "Yeah. Your neck, your boobs and even your pussy but I don't know if you want to go that far".

Emily felt like she was on fire when he said pussy.

She thought. *Guys actually kiss girls down there? This is news to me. That doesn't happen in any of the books that I read.*

Emily flushed.

Emily stammered. " Y-y-you would actually kiss me there".

Elijah squeezed her hand gently. "Well yeah. Normally I don't do that with girlfriends. Not that I expect you to be my girlfriend. It's just you are so different from my exes in a good way. I just want to treat you with respect, so I'm not going to force you to do anything you don't want to do".

Emily was so grateful that Elijah was a gentleman. She always wanted a guy who was chivalrous but Emily figured that boys like that no longer existed. She was so overcome with passion that she kissed him which Emily could tell took Elijah by surprise.

After pulling away, Emily responded.

"You can start by kissing my neck. Maybe by the third date you can kiss my boobs. I would love to be your girlfriend. You are just the sweetest guy ever. I'm so attracted to you that I am controlling myself too. I don't want to go too fast either. Let's go slow but not too slow".

Elijah was stunned. For a girl that had not been with a guy sexually she sure knew how to rev his engines. Who knew being nice to a girl could lead to her making out with you? He started to kiss her neck slowly and then he kissed her cheeks, nose, forehead leading his lips to hers again. Elijah couldn't get enough of kissing her. He heard her moan when they were kissing and it took everything in him not to get on top of her right then and there and fuck her brains out. He was glad that she wanted to have sex with him too. He could tell her desire by the way she kissed him. Then without him even showing her what to do she started kissing him on the neck going all the way up to his forehead and back to his lips. He realized that Emily was a quick learner and Elijah liked that.

Elijah was surprised."How did you even know how to do that? Did you just follow what I did?''

Emily was smiling."I kind of followed you and I read romance books. I just went with what the female character does."

He put his hands through her hair.

Elijah grinned."I should have known that you read romance books. Let me guess I'm the one that has Fabio on the cover?"

Emily laughed.

Emily started touching his hair.'No. I don't read those kinds of romance books. They are cheesy even for me."

Elijah just kept kissing her. He looked at his watch and realized that it was 10 pm.

Elijah sighed. "Damn. We have been here for a very long time. I guess I should take you home now".

Emily pouted. "It doesn't even feel like it has been that long. This is going to sound weird and corny. I feel like I have known you for a long time even though we just met yesterday".

Elijah grinned. "I feel the same way Emily''.

Emily has a surprised look on her face. "You do?''

Elijah smiled. "Yes I do. There is just something about you that I can't put a finger on. I do want to one day put my hands all over you".

Elijah could tell that Emily was wet just by looking at her facial expression. He held her for a few minutes while stroking her back. She purred like a kitten. They went right back to kissing. He lost track of how many times he and Emily had kissed. Elijah loved kissing her and her reaction to it gave his penis blue balls. He knew when he got home tonight, he had to rub one out. Eventually Elijah and Emily stopped kissing. They talked for a few more minutes before they made their way back to the car. He dropped her off at her house and kissed her again. Elijah didn't want to seem eager, but he wanted to see her tomorrow.

Elijah asked. "Are you doing anything tomorrow?"

Emily smiled big and his cock was rock hard.

Emily responded while holding his hand. "I'm not doing anything tomorrow. I don't really go out. I'm kind of a homebody."

Elijah was surprised." Really? I'm the opposite. I love to go out. I had a great time tonight by the way".

Emily smiled at Elijah."So did I. I will see you tomorrow then. You can text me the details in the morning".

Elijah liked how confident she was.

Elijah parked the car and looked at Emily. "Sounds good Emily''.

He kissed the palm of her hand and closed her fingers.

Elijah grinned. "That way you dont forget about me".

Emily smiled back."Please Elijah. Like I could ever forget you".

He gave her one last kiss and then she got out of the car.

Elijah waited until she was inside her house to leave.

She gave him a wave and he waved back before pulling out of the driveway.

When he got home, Elijah jerked off. He thought about kissing Emily's breasts while squeezing them. His orgasm was massive and made his whole body shake.

He thought.*This has never happened to me before. What is it about this girl that causes me to have intense orgasms? I'm not sure but I am definitely not letting her go. I can't wait until tomorrow.*

Chapter 6

Emily woke up feeling refreshed. She got a text from Elijah.

"Hi Emily. How do you feel about paintball?" Emily texted back. "Hi Elijah. I would love to do paintball." Emily smiled and texted back. "Hi Elijah. I would love to do paintball." Elijah sent. "Great. How about I pick you up at 1?" Emily replied. "Sounds good. See you then." Elijah texted. "I probably shouldn't say this but I masturbated last night and thought of you." Emily was shocked. She sent. "You did? I masturbated too."

Elijah texted. "Wait you masturbated as well. Who did you think of?"

Emily thought. *Should I tell him?* She decided to be honest. "You." Elijah replied. "You thought of me?"

Emily grinned. "Yes."

Elijah responded. "That just turns me on".

Emily was curious. "Really?"

Elijah retorted. "Yeah. I'd better stop texting you before I start mentioning other sexual things".

Emily replied. "Like what?"

Elijah sent. "You are not ready for that yet Emily".

Emily responded. "I have a vibrator. My friend Sam helped me get it".

Elijah sent in all caps." WOW. I did not expect that. You surprise me Emily".

Emily asked. "In a good way?"

Elijah retorted, "In the best way. I have to go. John, Jason and Samuel want to do darts."

Emily countered. "Good luck."

Elijah sent. "Thanks Emily. See you at 1."

Emily replied. "See you at 1 Elijah."

They stopped texting each other and Emily called Sam. "Sam I had the most amazing first date with Elijah. Now he tells me that he masturbated while thinking about me."

Sam was shocked. "Wow Em. This guy really likes you. What did you guys do anyway?"

Emily smiled. "We went to Olive Garden and looked at the stars".

Sam curiously asked. "Em, did you tell him to take you to those places?"

Emily responded. "No. He just came up with those ideas on his own."

Sam wanted to know more. "That's great Em. Did you kiss him?"

Emily answered. " Yes. Well he kissed me first and then I kissed him. He even kissed me on the neck".

Sam gasped. "Wow Em. That sounds scandalous. I'm proud of you for getting kissed on the neck".

Emily grinned. "Thanks Sam. We are going on another date today."

Sam replied. "What are you two love birds going to do?"

Emily retorted while having a big smile on her face. "We are going to do paintball."

Sam sighed. "Make sure to throw yourself on top of him and kiss him some more."

Sam gave Emily tips on kissing guys including french kissing.

After a long conversation with Sam, Emily got ready for the day. She watched some cartoons. In the back of her mind, she thought. *I finally found a guy who actually likes me and wants to treat me right. Thank you God for helping me find someone who cares about me. Now I just have to be myself around him which won't be too hard. He brings out the best version of me.*

Elijah called up his friends to talk about his first date with Emily. "We kissed and I think that she could be the one guys." Samuel, John and Jason sang in unison "Go Elijah." He laughs. "Thanks guys." Elijah talked to them about Star Trek before meeting Emily for paintball.

Elijah picked Emily up for paintball. He couldn't believe that she said yes to a second date with him. Once Emily was in his car, Elijah put his arm around her. He kissed her. One day had passed since he had seen her but he still missed her. She still brought so much passion into kissing. After a few minutes passed, he stopped kissing her   and   drove   towards   Paintball   Heaven.

Chapter 7

Emily smiled when they got to Paintball Heaven. Elijah showed her how to play paintball. "What you need to do is aim your paintball gun at the target until you hit your mark". Emily nodded her understanding, aimed her paintball gun and fired at Elijah. Elijah was caught off guard. ''Hey!"

Emily smirked. "Sorry Elijah. I guess the student surpassed the teacher." Elijah bowed at her. "You have learned well young grasshopper". They both started laughing and hitting each other with the paintball guns. Then they started making out. Several hours later, they started heading towards Elijah's car. They got into his car. Emily looked at Elijah."Thanks so much for today Elijah. I had so much fun." Elijah drove back to Emily's house. "You are welcome Emily. So I will see you tomorrow at school?" Emily grinned. "Yes you will Elijah. Have a good night.'' Elijah looked at Emily with love in his eyes." You have a good night too Emily."

They kissed and then Emily went into her house and rubbed one out before she went to sleep.

Elijah went home with a smile on his face. He had so much fun playing paintball with Emily today. He couldn't wait until the day he gave her so much pleasure that she would scream his name in ecstasy. Elijah knew that when that day came, he would be patient and supportive. He would cherish and nourish her like a flower. Elijah couldn't resist masturbating and thinking of cuming all over Emily's boobs. In seconds he came with semen bursting out of his penis. He then went to sleep with a smile on his face.

Chapter 8

Emily couldn't believe that her and Elijah have been going out for 5 months. She is so thankful that she met him. He makes her feel brave and confident in her own skin. She has never met anyone like him. He is sweet, caring and compassionate. He actually cares about her. Emily has been debating on whether she is ready to have sex with Elijah. She doesn't want their relationship to move too fast but she also knows that Elijah would make their first time very special. If he asks tonight if she wants to have sex Emily will say yes. She is terrified that she will not know what to do but Emily trusts Elijah to help her feel good. Emily wants her first time to be with Elijah because he is the greatest guy that she has ever met. No other guy would look at her with so much love like Elijah does. She recognizes that Elijah will treat her with respect and will not force her to do things that she would not want to do sexually. While Emily was deep in thought, Sam came up to her in the hallway.

"Em, what are you thinking about so intently?''

Emily faced Sam. "Sam. I need to talk to you about something."

Sam has a confused look on her face. "What is it Em? I know that you are not pregnant because you and Elijah have not had sex yet."

Emily pulls Sam to her locker and opens it so they can have a private conversation.

Emily puts her arm around Sam. "That's what I want to talk to you about Sam. I think I'm ready to have sex with Elijah."

Sam's mouth drops open. "Whoa Em this is huge news. No wonder you wanted to talk. I am so proud of you."

Emily smiled. "Thanks Sam. I just don't know how I am going to do it."

Sam gestured with her hands."Well Em. You find his penis and put it in your vagina."

Emily laughed. ''That's not what I mean, Sam. I want to make our first time special. Maybe we could go to his place and have candles lit. That would be romantic."

Sam sighs. "Oh Em. You don't need all of that. All you need is Elijah, a bed and a condom."

Emily frowns. "That's not romantic Sam. You know I love romance Sam, I always have."

Sam has an exasperated look on her face. "Yes I know Em. I should have known that you would want candles for your first time. What's next, rose petals on the bed?''

Emily interjected. "Actually Sam, that would be great. Should I tell Elijah that I am ready or should I surprise him?''

Sam smiled. '' I have an idea, Em. How do you feel about lingerie?''

Emily asked. "What's lingerie?''

Sam pouted "Oh Em. Lingerie is a girl's best friend."

Emily was confused. "I thought that was diamonds."

Sam shook her hand at Emily."No Em. Diamonds are what guys buy you if they want to lock you down. Lingerie is something that girls wear when they want to have sex with their boyfriends."

Emily wanted to know."Is it risque?"

Sam grinned."Of course Em. But I bet you that if you wore lingerie before you have sex with Elijah, he will want to take it off."

Emily gasped with her mouth open. "Wow. Really?"

Sam smirked. "Really girl. Guys love that shit. They love seeing you wearing something that shows all of your skin. Trust me Em. Elijah will want to have sex with you right then and there if you want to wear lingerie."

Emily wondered."Can you help me find something after school?"

Sam winked. "Of course Em. That's what best friends are for."

Then the warning bell started for first period English.

Emily sighed."I'd better go. You know that I don't like to be late for class."

Sam frowned. "True Em. You are weird like that but I love you."

Emily smiled."I love you too Sam."

They share a hug. Emily got her book, closed her locker and went to English while Sam goes to Math.

She thought. *I can't believe that I am going to get lingerie. If what Sam said is true, then I'm looking forward to Elijah taking it off. Note to self: get lingerie after school. Hopefully Elijah will have rose petals and candles lit when I get there.*

Before the warning bell went off

Elijah can't believe that he has been with Emily for 5 months. He wants to do something special for her but can't think of anything except having sex with her. Elijah knows that she is not ready for that. He is not going to push her or force her to have sex with him. Elijah is not the kind of guy to compel a girl to make love if she is not ready. He will ask her tonight after school if she wants to have sex. If by some magical reason she does then he would need to buy condoms. He was in the hallway when his friends came up to him.

John interjected.''So Elijah, you and Emily have been going out for five months now.''

Jason sighed in annoyance."I think he realizes how long he has been with his lady friend John.''

Samuel asked. "The real question is when are you two going to fuck?''

Elijah groaned. ''Samuel, I don't know if she is ready."

Samuel shook his head. "Elijah, man, you just have to ask her. Don't you have English with her?''

Elijah frowned. "Yes but I don't know if I should ask her during class. Emily is the type that loves class. What if I distract her?''

Jason commented while stroking his chin. "You could write her a note. Doesn't Emily love when someone transcribes something on paper?''

Elijah agreed."You are right Jason. I could write her a note and see what she says."

John nodded his head."Sounds good Elijah."

Jason conceded."Well done young Elijah."

Samuel added.''Just make sure to ask if she likes it raw."

All four of them laughed in unison.

Then the warning bell rang.

Elijah sighed."I have to go guys. See you in Algebra."

John waved at Elijah. "See you then Elijah."

Jason moved his hand back and forth. "Goodbye for now my good friend."

Samuel interjected."Try to get her to give you a blow job tonight Elijah."

Elijah laughed on his way to English. While John went to Social Studies, Jason went to Biology and Samuel went to Geography.

He went inside to English class and saw Emily sitting in the front of the class as usual. Elijah sat behind her and started writing her a note.

Elijah: We have been going out for five months.The best five months of my life. Would you want to take the next step and make love with me tonight?'

He gave Emily the note. Elijah watched her read it and noticed that there was a smile on her face. He thought that was a good sign.

She gave him the note. He opened it and saw her reply.

Emily: I swear that we have the same minds. I was going to ask if you wanted to have sex tonight.

Elijah couldn't believe his eyes. He had to reread the note to make sure that Emily actually wrote those words.

He wrote back. You actually want to have sex? I thought that you weren't ready.

He gave it to Emily and she wrote back. I didn't know that I was until 10 minutes ago. I want our first time to be special though so I am going to get something.

Elijah and Emily passed the note back and forth.

Elijah read the note and he couldn't stop thinking about the few things that she wanted to get. *Did that mean that she wanted to get condoms? He was the guy in the relationship so he should get the condoms. What special things could she be getting? What do girls get for their first time? Elijah wasn't sure but he knew that he would find out tonight.*

He wrote back. <u>That sounds good. I'm glad that you want to make our first time special. How does 6 pm at my place sound?</u>

Emily: <u>Sounds good.</u>

Elijah turned and looked at Emily. "I can't believe that you actually want to have sex with me."

Emily smiled. "I have been thinking about it Elijah. Where we are in our relationship, I feel very comfortable with you, which is good. Sam is going to help me get something for tonight. Before you ask, it is not condoms. I was hoping that you would take care of that."

Elijah gasped. "Is it what I think it is?"

Emily looked at him."Depends. What do you think I am going to get?''

Elijah gestured with his hands making a circle. He whispers in Emily's ear. "Is it lingerie?''

He felt Emily's breathing quicken. She whispered back. "How did you know?''

Elijah moved back a few paces. "Most girls get lingerie when they are ready for the next step in their relationships with their boyfriends''.

Emily grinned. "You know me so well Elijah. Sam suggested it so I'm going to get some after school today."

Elijah smirked. "I can't wait to see what you get. I just want you to know that I am going to be super horny. "

Emily winked at him. "That is what I am hoping for".

Elijah dropped his mouth open in shock. "You don't act like you are a virgin Emily."

Emily smiled. "I am though Elijah. Which probably means that I am very pent up sex wise."

Elijah laughed. "Oh you are definitely worked up if you are thinking of buying lingerie."

Emily giggled, making his cock throb with desire. Then Mrs. Smith started talking about last night's reading. Which put a damper on his erection. "I guess we have to stop talking now."

Emily pouted, which was adorable. "Yes we do. I will see you at your place at 6 Elijah. "

Elijah grinned. "Sounds good Emily." He kissed her forehead.

Elijah saw Emily blush at that. She smiled. "You are the sweetest guy that I have ever met Elijah."

He winked at her. "I'm glad that I make you happy Emily." Elijah blew her a kiss and turned to face Mrs. Smith. His hard on was back and he couldn't wait to make love to Emily tonight.

Emily could not stop grinning. She could not believe that Elijah blew her a kiss and kissed her forehead. He was such a compassionate, kind and caring person. She could not wait to be intimate with him tonight. Emily wanted him to kiss her all over her body until she shook with pleasure. She was ready to give him her flower. A girl's vagina was a very sacred place and she was excited to have Elijah enter her with his cock. Emily knew that it would hurt but she knew that he would make her first time special. She went through the rest of English class with a huge smile on her face. *Tonight I will become a woman.*

After English, Elijah met up with his friends in Algebra. They sat down in their seats. Samuel asked. "So did she say yes to you fucking her tonight?"

Elijah smiled. "Surprisingly yes. She even is getting some lingerie with her friend Sam after school."

Samuel high fived Elijah. "That's what I'm talking about. Now what you need to do is bang her so hard that she wants to keep going."

Elijah laughed. "Samuel I'm going to go slow with her. If she wants me to go hard, then I will do that. I'm not going to force anything though. I respect women. Did you guys do the homework last night? No one called me for help so I figured that everyone understood the equations."

John nodded his head. "Yes Elijah. The math was pretty simple so we did not need your assistance this time. We do appreciate you taking time to give us support."

Jason added. " I agree with John, Elijah. You are such a great friend to us."

Samuel interjected. "They are right Elijah. You do so much."

Elijah smiled. "Thanks guys."

Mr. Williams started talking about polynomials and the guys realized that they needed to stop talking.

Elijah sighed. "I guess it's time to learn math. Talk to you guys after?"

"Of course Elijah." the fellas said in unison.

Elijah grinned. "Great.

They got through Algebra. Elijah was thinking about Emily the whole time and about how magical their night is going to be.

Emily met up with Sam in Social Studies and told her about her conversation with Elijah. "He was surprised that I wanted to have sex with him."

Sam contorted her face in confusion. "Can you blame him? You said it yourself that you don't normally buy lingerie."

Emily laughed. "I know but I love Elijah. You have to put yourself out there for romance Sam."

Sam arched her eyebrows. "Does he know that you love him Em?"

Emily pouted. "No. I have been scared to tell him. What if he doesn't feel the same way?"

Sam winked. "I'm pretty sure if he didn't feel the same way, he wouldn't want to have sex with you."

Emily laughed. "True Sam. I just don't want it to be awkward."

Sam was the one giggling now. "With you Em, it is going to be super awkward."

Emily nodded her head. "You are right about that Sam. I just want it to be special. With Elijah, I know that he is going to appreciate my body."

Sam looked confused. "Really? How do you know that?"

Emily smiled. "He is such a sweet guy. He is the type of boy that would ask if I wanted to do a certain sex position. That is why I love him. Some guys wouldn't care about getting a girl's permission about sex. Elijah is different though."

Sam shook her head. "Yeah I know. You told me that he kissed your hand before. Most guys don't do that."

Emily smiled. "That is why Elijah is a great guy Sam. He is not like other boys."

Sam winked. "He is definitely your type of guy, Em. I hope that you have so much fun tonight."

Emily smirked. "Thanks Sam. I am totally going to enjoy myself tonight when Elijah and I fuck."

Sam gasps. "I am so glad that you are starting to swear, Emily. Maybe Elijah is a good influence on you or maybe it's me." Sam points at herself with glee.

Emily laughs. "Oh Sam. You are so funny."

They finished with Social Studies and the rest of their classes, with Emily grinning throughout the day.

7 hours later

Emily and Sam climbed into Emily's car at the end of the school day. Emily clapped her hands. "I can't believe that I am going to say this but I'm excited to buy lingerie."

Sam smiled. "Don't worry Emily. I will help you find the perfect nightwear to turn Elijah on."

Emily gave Sam a high five. "I know you will Sam. I trust you."

Sam snapped her fingers. "Let's go to the lingerie store. "

Emily smiled. "Sounds good Sam."

They went to the lingerie store. Emily got a cute purple night wear outfit. She thanked Sam again for helping her. "I really appreciate you helping me Sam."

Sam winked. "It's the least I could do. I want to make sure that at least someone is getting action tonight."

Emily and Sam giggled all the way to Emily's house. Emily dropped Sam off. "Don't do anything I wouldn't do Em."

Emily smirked. " I wouldn't dream of it Sam."

Emily drove the rest of the way to her house.

She got out, walked to her front door and went into her house with a big grin on her face. *I can't wait to fuck Elijah tonight.*

Elijah was excited to see Emily in a few hours. On the way to the parking lot after school, Elijah talked to Samuel. "Tonight is going to be magical Samuel." Samuel put his finger in his hand that is shaped like a circle. "Oh yeah it will. Just remember Elijah. Please do everything that I would do." Elijah laughed. "I will keep that in mind Samuel." He got into his car waving to Samuel. "See you on Monday Samuel." Samuel moved his hand back and forth. "Sounds good Elijah." He saw Samuel walk and get into his car. Elijah drove to the store. He knew that Emily wanted their first time to be special. Elijah bought condoms, candles and rose petals and went home with a smile on his face.

Emily got ready to go to Elijah's house. She put on the lingerie underneath her regular clothes. She put her coat on and went downstairs. Emily went outside to her car and drove to Elijah's house. Emily rang the doorbell. She saw Elijah's face when he opened the door. He looked surprised to see her just wearing a shirt and jeans. "Where is the lingerie?''

Emily smirked. "It's underneath my clothes."

She saw Elijah's eyes bug out of his head. Emily laughed. "I was hoping that was your reaction."

She noticed Elijah's smile. " You surprise me Emily.After you, my lady."

Emily smiled. "Thank you kind sir."

She walked into Elijah's house and up the stairs to his room with him following behind. Emily made it to Elijah's room and opened the door. She gasped. He had lit candles and placed rose petals on the bed. Emily started to smile. She turned toward Elijah. "How did you know I wanted this?"

Elijah grinned. "Well I know that this is your first time and you wanted it to be special. I decided to show you how romantic I can be."

Emily laughed. "Elijah, I already knew that you were romantic when you wanted to look at the stars on our first date. That's why I love you."

Elijah gasped. "You love me? That's crazy because I love you too."

Emily was shocked. "You do?"

Elijah nodded his head. "Yes. I was afraid that you didn't feel the same way."

Emily pouted. "Awww Elijah. Of course I feel the same way. I had the same fear. "

She walked right up to Elijah, took off her coat and kissed him. After they were done kissing, Emily started to take off her shirt and then her jeans. The surprised look on Elijah's face was worth any insecurity or embrassment that she might have had. She shook her body. "Aren't you going to get undressed too?" He quickly took off his clothes and guided her to the bed. Emily smiled as Elijah placed her on the bed. *I am excited for Elijah to pluck my flower.*

Elijah gently got on top of Emily. He kissed her forehead, cheeks, neck and then her breasts. "Elijah please stop teasing me." Elijah laughed as he moved to her stomach, thighs and legs. He then went back up to her vagina. Elijah wanted Emily to feel pleasure for her first time. He placed a condom on his dick. Then Elijah put his penis inside her vagina and started to thrust. She started to scream. At first he thought that she was screaming in pain. Elijah stopped moving inside her. "Are you okay Emily?'' He was surprised when he saw Emily smile. "Why did you stop?'' He was confused. " I thought that you were in pain." Emily grinned. "I knew that it would hurt but I also liked it when you moved inside me." Elijah smiled. " Do you want me to keep going?'' Emily smirked. "Yes please Elijah." Elijah liked that she was so polite. He started moving inside her again. Emily started screaming his name which Elijah liked a lot. "Oh Elijah, you are so good at this." He kept going. Elijah went deeper and he saw Emily gasp. He liked that she was vocal during sex. Elijah put his arms around her. Emily kept yelling. He felt her cum and then he came. Elijah knew that he had been with other girls but making love to Emily was a beautiful experience. Afterwards, they slept holding each other.

Chapter 9

The next morning

Emily felt rejuvenated. All of these years, she thought that she didn't need someone to hold her while she slept. Emily was wrong though. After a period of time where she did not know a man's touch, finally the waves of womanhood have washed over her. Emily was no longer a child. She looked at Elijah and kissed his chest. He woke up and kissed her lips. "Good morning beautiful. How are you feeling?" Emily smiled. "I feel amazing. I am a brand new person." Elijah smirked. "I'm glad. By the way, I am going to have to clean my sheets now." Emily blushed. "I'm sorry about that." Elijah laughed. "It's okay Emily. I expected that you would bleed. That's what happens when girls have sex for the first time." Now it was Emily's turn to giggle. "True Elijah. Do you need help to clean the sheets?" Emily saw Elijah grin at her. "No. You do not have to assist me with the cleaning. I can do it myself. Thank you for offering though." Emily got off the bed and let Elijah clean his sheet. She looked at her body in the mirror. Emily saw her breasts that looked like they got bigger overnight. She gazed down at her vagina and noticed that it resembled a pink waterfall. Her most intimate place had become a pleasure filled wonderland that she did not want to leave. Emily was now officially a woman.She enjoyed making love to Elijah last night. He made her feel good. She wanted to do the same for him. When he came back from cleaning the sheets, Emily turned and walked to him. She got on her knees and started stroking his cock. "Emily you don't have to do this." Emily smiled."I know Elijah. I want to make you feel good." She kept moving her hand on his penis. Elijah came. "Aaaaaaaaaaaaaaaah". He grinned at Emily. "Thanks Emily." She smirked. "You are welcome Elijah. I am going to take a bath." Elijah beamed. "Sounds good Emily. I'm going to clean up." Emily went to wash her hands and take a relaxing bath.

Elijah cleaned himself up while Emily took her bath. He got dressed and thought of how he was going to ask Emily to prom. Elijah knew that she liked romantic gestures. He will give her a pink rose. That will be very tender for her. Elijah shouted over the water "Emily I'm going to go to the store real quick." He heard her say "Okay. Sounds good, my love." Elijah smiled when she said that. "Okay. See you in 10 minutes." He walked out of the house and got into his car. Elijah went to the store and bought a pink rose for Emily. He drove back to his house and went inside. Elijah knocked on the bedroom door. "Are you decent?" Emily yelled out "yes I am dressed." With that, he strided into the bedroom with the rose behind his back. "I have something for you Emily." What is it?" she asked with curious eyes. "First I want to ask you a question?" He pulled the rose from behind his back. "Will you go to prom with me Emily?" Emily grinned. Elijah knew that he did the right action to make her smile. "Yes, of course I want to go to the prom with you Elijah." He smirked, pulled her into his arms and kissed her. *I am going to marry this girl one day.*

Chapter 10

2 months later

Prom was here and Emily was so excited. She got ready with Sam. "I am so glad that I have someone to go to prom with." Emily smiled. Sam smirked. "Yep, Em. All of those years reading books and doing homework actually paid off." Emily laughed. "Haha, Sam. You are so funny. Who are you going with?" Sam shrugged. "I'm not sure yet Em. All I know is the world is my oyster." She smiled while Sam put on makeup. *That is such a Sam thing to say. I hope she finds someone like I found Elijah.* "Well Sam. I hope you find some guy who has as much sense of humor as you do." Sam winked. "One can only hope Emily." They both giggled while Emily put on her dress and brushed her hair. *I can't wait to dance with Elijah tonight. This prom is going to be so amazing.*

Elijah put on his blue suit and got ready for prom with John, Jason and Samuel. "I'm actually happy to go to a dance guys." He gave his friends high fives. Samuel nodded his head. "You should be Elijah. You and Emily have been together for a while. I only hope that I can find someone that I can get along with." Elijah smiled. "You will find a girl Samuel. Who knows? Maybe there could be someone out there that makes dirty jokes." Jason shook his head. "Samuel has a rare indecent mind that few could replicate." John agrees. "Jason is right, Elijah. Not many people could stomach Samuel's dirty jokes let alone say them." They all laugh. Elijah snaps his fingers. "I have to pick up Emily but I will see you guys there." Him and his friends did a fist bump. "Sounds good Elijah. Make sure to dance real close to Emily." Samuel gestured with his hands. "Oh Samuel." Elijah, John and Jason said in unison. Elijah got a corsage for Emily and drove to her house while his friends got in their cars. He was excited to dance with Emily tonight.

Emily waved goodbye to Sam as she got into her car. As Sam left, Elijah pulled up in his car to pick her up. Emily smiled. Elijah had gotten her a purple corsage which went with her purple and black butterfly dress. "Thank you so much Elijah." Elijah was the one to grin. "You are welcome Emily." He kissed her and the excitement of going to prom hit her like a ton of bricks. They came apart and she closed the door and got into Elijah's car with him. When her and Elijah got to prom, Emily was grinning like a fool. She quickly gasped though when she saw Sam and Elijah's friend Samuel making out. "I did not realize that Sam would be into one of your friends." Elijah did not look shocked. "Honestly, the way you talk about Sam being a huge flirt it makes sense to me." Emily laughed. "That is true. I just did not think that they knew each other. " Elijah makes a weird face. "They definitely know each other very well now." Emily was wondering what he was talking about. She turned around and realized that they were humping each other. Before Elijah and Emily knew it, a slow song came on. She saw Elijah put out his hand. "May I have this dance?" Emily blushed. "I don't know how to slow dance Elijah." He smiled. "It's okay, Emily. I will teach you." Emily put her hand in Elijah's and they both started to sway back and forth. She couldn't stop staring into Elijah's eyes the whole time they danced. Emily noticed that he was looking into her eyes the whole time too. *I never want to forget this feeling. I hope that Elijah and I stay together forever.*

Chapter 11

2 weeks later

Graduation was here and Elijah was feeling sad. He had gotten into MIT which was his dream school. Unfortunately, it was 310 miles away from Emily. She was going to go to Carnegie Mellon and get her creative writing degree. Elijah was going to miss her but he knew that he needed to go to MIT in order to be the best engineer there was. He put on his cap and gown and drove to Glennbrook one last time. When Elijah got there, he found his friends and gave them all a big bear hug. "I can't believe that we are all going to go to different colleges." Samuel squeezed Elijah, John and Jason. "I am going to miss you guys." John tried to wriggle out from under Samuel. "I would like to get out of this hug now Samuel." Jason was struggling to get out as well. "I would very much like to escape too dear Samuel." Samuel shrugged and let them go. "You guys are no fun." They all laughed and went to their seats. Elijah sat next to Emily. He held her hand. "How are you feeling?" Elijah saw Emily smile. "I'm excited but also nervous. " He rubbed her hand in circles with his hands. "You are going to be great at Carnegie Mellon. I believe in you." She beamed. "Thanks Elijah." He kissed her. "You are welcome Emily." *I am going to miss her so much when I go to college.*

Emily waited for her name to be called. "Emily Applebaum" could be heard from the principal. She stood up and received her diploma. As Emily turned, she saw Elijah and Sam cheer her on. They both screamed "go Emily." She smirked while walking down the platform back to her seat. Other people were called. Then she heard "Samantha Smith." When Sam was selected, Emily encouraged her. "Go Sam." She clapped her hands for Sam. Elijah's friend John was called. "John Carpenter." Elijah, Jason and Samuel clapped for him. Soon it was Elijah's turn to get his diploma. "Elijah Henderson" was shouted by the administrator. Elijah got up and received his diploma. Emily screamed so loud "I love you so much Elijah Henderson. I am so proud of you." He turned around and blushed. *I am going to miss him when I go to college.*

Elijah walked back down to his chair. Samuel's turn came. "Samuel Parks." Elijah, John and Jason screamed "go Samuel." Samuel yelled "so long motherfuckers" while getting his diploma. All of the graduates in the auditorium laughed. Jason's turn came. "Jason Walker." Elijah, John and Samuel did the wave. Elijah kissed Emily. "I am going to miss you like crazy Emily." She put her hand in his. "I am going to miss you too." He put his arm around her. "We are going to text and call each other everyday." Emily smiled. "Yes we will Elijah. I love you." "I love you too Emily." They kissed. *I want Emily and I to always be together hopefully.*

Chapter 12

3 months later

Emily settled into her dorm at Carnegie Mellon. She missed Elijah but she knew that he had to go to MIT to follow his dreams. They saw each other every once in a while. Emily felt so lonely that she used her vibrator to masturbate. She was so sad that she listened to "This isn't the end" by Owl city. Emily sat in bed just staring at the ceiling. *I can't wait until I see Elijah again.*

Elijah was at MIT missing Emily so much. He called and texted her when he wasn't busy with his classes or homework. Elijah passed the time when he wasn't caught up in schoolwork and talking to Emily, jerking off. He craved her touch and gentle embrace. *I can't wait to see Emily again.*

6 months later

Emily was excited to see Elijah. Their relationship has been very difficult these past six months. She couldn't wait to hold him in her arms. Emily heard a knock on her door. "Knock knock." She opened the door and ran into Elijah's biceps. "I am so glad that you are here Elijah." "I'm happy to be here Emily." They sat on Emily's bed and talked for a few hours. Things got heated though. "I miss seeing you Elijah." His face got really red. "You think I don't miss seeing you Emily?" Emily started raising her voice. "That is not what I meant and you know that." Elijah yelled "I try to see you as much as I can Emily." She fired back "it's not enough Elijah. I need you to be there for me when I am feeling sad." The argument went back and forth. "I am there for you, Emily." "I need you more Elijah. I feel you pulling away when we video chat." "I could say the same about you Emily." "I don't do that Elijah." "YES YOU DO EMILY." "NO I DON'T Elijah." Elijah's hands grew tense."I KNOW THAT YOU HAVE BEEN SEEING SOMEONE." Emily's hands turned rigid. "I HAVE NOT BEEN SEEING ANYONE." "THEN WHY ARE YOU ACTING LIKE THIS?'' "ACTING LIKE WHAT?" "LIKE A CRAZY BITCH." "I AM NOT CRAZY AND I AM NOT A BITCH." Elijah stomped his feet." I CAN'T DEAL WITH THIS RIGHT NOW." Emily pointed to the door."THEN GO." Elijah fumed with anger. "FINE. GOODBYE EMILY." He walked to the door. "GOODBYE ELIJAH." Elijah walked out, slamming the door. Emily started balling her eyes out and put on Taylor Swift. Listening to "White Horse", she sobbed hysterically. Emily cried herself to sleep. *I feel like my heart just broke into a million pieces.*

Elijah drove home trying hard not to cry. *You are a man Elijah. You are not going to cry.* He started to weep. *I can't believe that Emily and I are over. My heart feels like it has been crushed and smashed. How am I going to get through the rest of college? I will figure it out somehow. Be strong Elijah.* He made it to his dorm room and cried throughout the night.

Chapter 13

Emily had not seen Elijah in two years.Since the break up, she has taken time to work on getting her Creative Writing degree. Emily tried going on a few dates but none of the guys made her feel any sparks. She mainly went to classes and did her homework. Emily graduated with her Bachelor's degree in Creative Writing. When she looked out at the audience though, she wished that Elijah was there. Emily realized that the distance drove them apart. She wished that she could call him but Emily knew that he wouldn't want to hear from her. She went through her days, until she got a ticket to an All Time Low concert in Philly. Emily attended the concert and was listening to "Remembering Sunday" when someone tapped her on the shoulder. "Emily is that you?'' She turned around and gasped. Elijah was right behind her. *I can't believe that he is here in front of me.*

Elijah was stunned. He had not seen Emily in 2 years and now she was right there. The past few years have been rough on him. He went on dates with women but they just didn't attract him. Elijah still missed Emily as he was finishing his Engineering degree. He wanted to text her or call her so bad. The way things ended though, he figured that she hated him. Now she was near him and it took everything in him not to hold her and kiss her. He wasn't mad at her anymore. Long-distance relationships don't last. Elijah should have known that their bond could be broken by separation. He wanted to be with Emily again even if it meant that there was a possibility that they wouldn't be together in the long run. Elijah had hope that this time would be different. He heard Emily start to talk. "Elijah? How are you here? What are the odds?" Elijah twisted his hands. He was full of nerves. "I just came to see All time Low in concert. I didn't know that you would be here. I'm glad that I came though. I missed you." *Maybe I shouldn't have said that. What if she didn't miss me?* Elijah saw that her mouth gaped in shock. She quickly composed herself. "I missed you too. I tried to get over you but it's hard to forget about the first guy that made me have a huge orgasm during sex. I haven't been with anyone since we broke up." Now it was his turn to have his mouth drop open. "Y-y-you haven't had sex with anyone?" Emily laughed. "I thought I told you when we first started going out that I would only have sex with one person." Elijah sighed. "I didn't think that you were actually serious." She had a sarcastic look on her face. "When am I not serious Elijah?'' She had a point there. "I haven't had sex with anyone either. No one compares to you." He dipped her and kissed her. Elijah felt her kiss him back and he knew that everything was going to be okay with them.

Chapter 14

6 months later

Emily moved in with Elijah a few weeks ago. She was in shock months ago when she bumped into him. Emily was happy though that he actually missed her. She couldn't believe that they were together again. Emily wrote short stories and Elijah worked as a mechanical engineer in a factory. They spent their nights cuddling up on the couch and watching movies. She loved spending time with him. Emily was not going to jinx this. She was going to take life one step at a time. *God really does work in mysterious ways.*

Elijah was so glad that Emily lives with him. He looked forward to seeing her when he got done work. Elijah would cook dinner for her and they would watch tv. After tv, they would fuck their brains out. He would cum inside her and she would scream his name. *God I missed her so much. No other woman fucks like she does.* Afterwards, he laid in bed with his arm around her.

Emily has been with Elijah for a year now since they broke up. She was surprised that he wanted to take her out to a fancy restaurant. They had not done that since their first date. She wanted to hope that he was going to propose. Emily didn't want to get her hopes up though just in case he wasn't going to pop the question. They got to their table and Elijah pulled the chair out for her reminding Emily of their first date. She sat in her chair and they ordered their food. As they ate their food, Emily still wondered what was going to happen next. After her and Elijah had their dinner, he ordered her a peanut butter chocolate dream bar which was Emily's favorite. Her suspicions grew. When her dessert came out and the waiter placed it on the table, she saw Elijah kneel down. He brought out a ring box from his pocket. "Emily Rose Applebaum, will you give me the pleasure of being my wife?" Emily gasped and started crying happy tears. "Yes, yes a million times yes." Elijah stood up, brought Emily out of her seat and kissed her. *I am so glad that I get to spend the rest of my life with him.*

Elijah was relieved that she said yes. *Thank god I planned this months in advance.* He stopped kissing her and they shared the dessert. Elijah drove him and Emily home. They made love and he felt Emily's passion increase as he thrusted into her. Him and Emily came at the same time both with smiles on their faces. They went to sleep with love in their hearts.

Chapter 15

4 months later

There were two weeks until the wedding and Emily was ecstatic. She was at Amelia's Bridals with Sam picking out a dress. "Sam, what do you think about this one?" Emily twirled around the room. Sam frowned. "I think you are trying too hard with that one Em. Remember that it's going to be a small wedding. You don't have to wear a fancy dress that is going to be overflowing on you. Just find one that works for you." Emily smiled. "You know me so well Sam. Thanks for being my maid of honor." Sam grinned and gave her a hug. "You are welcome Em. I'm so glad that I get to be a part of your special day." They stopped hugging and Emily grinned. "I am happy that you are going to be there Sam." She tried on a few more dresses. Emily came out of the dressing room twinkling with glee. "This is the one Sam. I can feel it in my bones." She had on a purple dress with butterflies on the front. Sam looked at the dress. "Em, that is so you." Emily smiled. "I know right? I don't even care that it isn't white. This dress feels so comfortable and it is beautiful." Sam smirked. "You look great in it Em and I bet that Elijah will love taking it off you." Emily laughed. "Yes, he certainly will." She went back into the dressing room, took off the dress and changed into her clothes. Sam looked for a maid of honor dress and paid for the gown.

Emily went to the register and paid for her dress. Sam and her left the store and talked about penises.

Elijah was at Louis's Tuxes with John, Jason and Samuel trying to find a suit for the wedding. "Thanks so much for coming with me guys." John was picking out suits for him. "Of course Elijah. You know that we are here for you." He handed Elijah the suits to try on. "I really appreciate it John." Jason chimed in "We are so happy for you Elijah. You are so v-" Samuel interrupted "Thankfully you are finally locking this shit down." Jason was upset. "Samuel, I was talking. I was going to say to Elijah, that he is so very lucky to have a woman like Emily." Elijah smiled. " I know Jason. I am so glad that she and I were able to reconnect after 2 years of being apart. Honestly, the separation made our love stronger than ever. Us being able to take time apart and then come back together is a miracle. I didn't think that it would happen after the breakup. I am so glad that it did though, because now I love Emily as much as I did in high school. I love her even more actually. She has grown so much and so have I through the years." Samuel put his arm around Elijah. "You deserve to be happy Elijah." He smiled. "You are right Samuel." All three of his friends pushed him playfully into a changing room stall. Their voices shouted in unison "Let's get you into a suit." After trying on several suits, Elijah came out of the dressing room with a red tuxedo on. "This is the suit that I should wear. The tuxedo fits and I can breathe in it, which is a good thing." His friends laughed. Samuel gestured with his hands. "Of course it's a good thing that you can breathe in the suit. That way, Emily can take it off you when you guys fuck afterward." Jason sighed. "Oh Samuel. You and your dirty thoughts." John chimed in "Now that Elijah has found his suit, let's find our tuxedos." The three of them tried on suits while Elijah paid for his. After they all got their suits, the friends went to Elijah's house to play darts.

Day of the Wedding

Emily was so nervous. She felt so many butterflies in her stomach. Emily was in her and Elijah's apartment getting ready. Sam helped by fixing her train and reminding her to breathe. "Remember after today Em, you are going to be Mrs. Elijah Henderson." Emily smiled. "Thanks so much for calming me down Sam." Sam grinned. "You know that I am always here for you Emily." "I know Samantha." This time, Sam didn't get angry. Instead she smirked at Emily. "Welcome to the rest of your life Em." They hugged. After, Sam drove both of them to Rose Tree Park where the wedding would take place. *Today I am going to marry the love of my life. I can't wait to have his babies.*

Elijah was at the makeshift pew outside with John, Jason and Samuel. He had gotten ready at Samuel's house with the guys. Elijah didn't want either of them to have bad luck today. He waited for Emily to get here with Sam. Speaking of her, Elijah kept meaning to ask how she and Samuel met in high school. He knew that he had never introduced them. "So Samuel, how did you and Sam meet in high school?" Samuel sighed. "You are just asking me this now dude. High school was almost 6 years ago." Elijah put his hands up in a shrug. "Well, I kept meaning to ask you but then I would forget." Samuel rolled his eyes. "We met in the hallway. She bumped into me. I thought it was weird but then she was hot. I was not going to complain about an attractive girl crashing into me." Elijah laughed. "Only you would meet Emily's friend in the hallway of our high school. " Samuel smiled. "Yeah. She has been a pain in my side ever since." Elijah gasped. "Wait, you guys are still going out? You normally stay in a relationship for two months with a girl." Samuel sighed. "Yeah I know, but Samantha is different from other women. We had our rough patches just like you and Emily. She really matured since high school and so have I. I'm not the same guy that I was when we started being friends Elijah. I am more sophisticated now." Elijah laughed. "Says the guy who still watches porn in his free time." Samuel giggled. "Well, that is the best hour to watch porn, when you are not busy doing anything. Plus don't tell me all guys don't watch porn, even you." Elijah smirked. "Okay fine. You got me there Samuel." He saw Samuel start to smile. Elijah looked ahead and noticed that Sam was walking up the aisle. He was happy for Samuel. Who knew that Emily's friend would like his friend? Sam went up the pew and started making out with Samuel. He did not realize that she was going to do that but then he heard the wedding march. Sam and Samuel stopped kissing. Elijah felt like his heart was beating so fast and he was breathless. Walking up the aisle was the most beautiful woman that he had ever seen. Elijah was so glad that she was going to be his wife. Emily looked radiant in her purple butterfly dress. She got up to where he was, looked at his suit and smiled. *I am the luckiest man in the world.*

Emily stood next to Elijah with a big grin on her face. He held her hands. The officiant started to speak, "we are gathered here today to join Emily Applebaum and Elijah Henderson in holy matrimony." They looked into each other's eyes and said their vows. Elijah was first. "I didn't know when I was 18 years old, that I would be standing here looking at my future wife. When I first met you,

you were awkward and shy. You stuttered when you first saw me. I thought, wow this girl is so adorable. From our first date to prom, I just started to fall in love with you. Then we went to college and hit a speed bump. Fate stepped in though and allowed us to be together again. I am so thankful to have you in my life Emily. You make me a better man than I was before I met you. I love you so much." Emily was next with tears in her eyes. "I did not know when love was until I found you. Years before we met, I would not talk to guys. Then when we started going out, I felt more comfortable with you. I could be myself with you. After a few months, I started to fall for you. You are the most amazing man that I have ever met. Elijah Henderson, you are such a sweet person. I can't wait to spend the rest of my life with you."

"I, Elijah Robert Henderson take Emily Rose Applebaum to be my lawfully wedded wife. To love and care for, to have and to hold, from this day forward, for better or for worse, for richer or for poorer, in sickness and in health until death do us part." Emily and Elijah smiled at each other. "I, Emily Rose Applebaum take Elijah Robert Henderson to be my lawfully wedded husband. To love and care for, to have and to hold, from this day forward, for better or for worse, for richer or for poorer, in sickness and in health until death do us part." They exchanged rings. The officiant boomed " Here are Mr. and Mrs. Elijah Henderson. I now pronounce you man and wife. Elijah, you may now kiss the bride." Elijah kissed her and Emily felt like she was on cloud nine. *Today starts the rest of my life.* She and Elijah slowly danced to "Lover" by Taylor Swift at their reception.She wanted to put her hands around his ass and squeeze it

but they were in public in the gazebo. They went to their apartment
after   and   had   sex.

Chapter 16

Emily was throwing up in the bathroom. She then sat on the toilet with a pregnancy test near her vagina. She peed on the stick and waited two minutes for the results. There were two little blue lines on the stick. "Holy fuck. ELIJAH I'M PREGNANT!!!!!!" Elijah ran into the bathroom. "You are pregnant? This is amazing. I can't believe that I am going to be a dad." Emily is putting her underwear back on and her pants, placing the test on the sink. She starts to cry. "I'm going to be a mom." Elijah hugged her. "You are going to be a great mom Emily." Emily smiled. "Thanks Elijah. I love you." He touched her hair. "I love you too Emily." They kissed and then got out of the bathroom. Emily and Elijah ate lunch and while they sat on the couch, he massaged her feet. *I am so glad that Elijah did not freak out when I told him. I can't wait to have a kid that looks like him.*

Elijah was so excited that Emily was going to have his baby. They were going to have a boy or a girl. He worried that he would not be a good father. However, Elijah knew that he and Emily would raise their son or daughter together. *I can't wait until her stomach gets fuller and her boobs get bigger. I want to kiss her belly as the baby grows inside her. She is going to be an amazing mother.*

Emily's stomach started growing. Her breasts were filled with milk. Elijah would kiss her belly and talk to the baby. He even learned lullabies to play on the acoustic guitar. Her days were filled with morning sickness where Elijah would hold back her hair while she threw up. Emily's feet would also hurt and he would rub her feet. *Elijah is such a great man. I fall more in love with him every day. He makes me feel like a queen.* When they would go to sleep, Elijah would place his hands on her protruding stomach as if to protect their future son or daughter. *He is going to be a great dad.*

Elijah sat in Doctor Singh's office with Emily to find out the gender of the baby. He held her hand as doctor Singh said, "Congratulations. You are going to have a boy." They looked at each other and smiled. "He is going to look just like you Elijah. I already know what to name him." Elijah decided to be funny. "Mortimer Khan." Emily laughed. *I still love it when she laughs.* "No, Elijah. We are not naming our son Mortimer Khan. Let's name him Louis." Elijah smirked. "You have been thinking about this for a while, haven't you Emily?'' Emily smiled. "Of course I have thought about this for a while Elijah. Do you not know me?" Elijah laughed. "Of course I know you, Emily. We have been married for 6 months and we have known each other for almost 7 years." Emily winked. " I love when you are sarcastic Elijah. " Doctor Singh chimed in, "if you two are done, I can show you some pictures of the baby." Elijah faced the doct "Of course." The doctor showed them pictures of their son. Emily couldn't stop crying and Elijah had a big shit-eating grin on his face.

Our son is going to learn how to be an engineer and learn how to play the guitar. I hope that he looks like Emily and is sweet like

73

her. When Emily was into her second trimester when Doctor Singh called them in for another ultrasound. Doctor Singh showed them the picture of the baby. "I know that I told you that you were going to have a boy but it looks like you are going to have a girl as well. How do you feel about having twins?" Elijah and Emily's jaws dropped. "How is this possible?" Emily asked. Doctor Singh replied, "sometimes the first ultrasound does not pick up the other child." Elijah looked confused. "How does that work?" Doctor Singh reassured them, "it happens in pregnancies when the other baby is hiding right behind the other one, so we are not able to detect from the first ultrasound. There is also a chance that your babies were so close together in the same sac, that the one twin was hard to see. " Elijah laughed. "Wow, I'm so fertile that I got you pregnant with two kids." They both giggled. Emily and Elijah looked at each other and smiled. They were going to have twins. Elijah and Emily made sure to get everything ready for the twin's arrival.

Emily was sitting with Elijah on the couch watching "Tangled" when she felt herself pee but it was actually water on the floor. "Fuck, Elijah. I am having these babies. My water just broke." She saw Elijah jump up from the couch, gently pick her up and put her in the car. He drove them to the hospital. Emily wasn't supposed to be due for a few more days, but they got the crib and diapers a few weeks ago. She liked to be prepared. He took her out of the car when they got to the hospital and put her in a wheelchair. Elijah wheeled her to a nurse and said "my wife's water just broke." The nurse took Emily and brought her to a room. She was feeling nervous in the hospital bed but she couldn't wait to meet her son. The doctor came in, got her on an epidural and she started pushing. After 8 hours,

Emily stopped pushing and two cries could be heard. Doctor Singh smiled. "Congrats Emily and Elijah. You have two healthy babies." "Can I please see them?'' Emily wanted to know. Doctor Singh nodded. "Of course, Emily." Doctor Singh placed the two babies in Emily's arms. Emily fell in love with both of them. They were so cute. The twins had brown hair. The girl had brown eyes and the boy had blue eyes. She hugged them and they immediately went to her breasts. Elijah laughed. "Well at least they have good taste." Emily chuckled. She started to breastfeed the twins. "I know what I want to call them Elijah." Elijah asked "what is that Emily?" She smiled. "Louis Richard Henderson and Amelia Michele Henderson." Elijah grinned. "Sounds good to me, Emily." He kissed her as Amelia and Louis kept sucking her boobs. *They are so beautiful. I can't wait to watch them grow up.*

Chapter 17

Elijah and Emily brought Amelia and Louis home from the hospital, a few weeks after they were born. Their days were spent changing diapers and getting them to go to sleep. Emily breastfed them. They had plenty of sleepless nights. As Emily and Elijah slept in their bed, the baby monitor started to make noise. They would take turns comforting the twins. Emily would sing to them and rock them, while Elijah would hold them. He got up this time, so Emily could get some rest. He went to the nursery, picked up Amelia and Louis and held them. *They are so small. I can't believe that they came out of Emily's vagina. Amelia and Louis don't even have hair yet. I can't wait to watch them grow up. I am still as in love with Emily as I was when we first met.*

Emily smiled as Elijah played the "play play funtime song" on his guitar for Amelia and Louis's first birthday party. She was so proud of him. He was such a great dad just like she knew he would be. Amelia and Louis both had brown hair now. They were walking around with her and looking at the cake. She remembered a few weeks ago when the twins started to walk. Elijah was cooking dinner for the two of them. She was picking up Louis to get him ready to eat his solid food, when Amelia started to walk towards her and Elijah. Emily put down Louis and then he started to walk to Elijah.

She felt such a proud feeling in her chest. Emily still thinks about that magic moment when she is feeling stressed about bills and the mortgage. Her and Elijah bought a house before the twins were born. They wanted Amelia and Louis to grow up in a house that was warm and spacious, not an apartment building. After Elijah was done playing, they helped Amelia and Louis blow out the candles. *I can't believe that they are one years old today. The twins are so cute. They look just like Elijah and me. I am so thankful to have them and Elijah in my life. I love him with all my heart.*

Elijah and Emily helped Amelia and Louis get ready for their first day of preschool. They were scared but Elijah and Emily helped calm them down. Elijah assisted Louis with getting dressed, while Emily supervised Amelia with getting changed. *Hopefully while the kids are at preschool, Emily and I can fuck. It has been so long since we last had sex.* Him and Emily dropped the twins off, and they had wild, passionate sex. When Emily was on top of him, he instantly got hard just like the good old days. The two of them had not had sex since the twins were born. She moved in rhythm against him and Elijah felt like he was going to cum at any moment. Emily rubbed her breasts on his chest and she started moaning. Elijah and Emily came at the same time. Afterwards, he held Emily in his arms. *I never get tired of having sex with her. She is an amazing goddess of fucking.*

Emily and Elijah took Amelia and Louis to their school for kindergarten. The twins were hesitant. They didn't think that they would make any friends. Her and Elijah assured them to just be themselves and not to worry what other people think. Emily and Elijah gave them a big hug. *They are growing up so fast. I can't believe that they are in kindergarten now. Soon they will be teenagers and then adults getting their driver's licenses. Time flies by. Elijah is the most amazing man that I have ever met.*

Elijah and Emily continued to take care of Amelia and Louis through elementary school, middle school and high school. Amelia was like her mother. She got good grades and did her homework. Louis on the other hand was like his dad. He was hyper and he enjoyed playing video games. Elijah and Emily were now in their 40's watching the twins graduate high school. Elijah thought *wow I still remember when they were in diapers, and Emily and I were changing them. They develop so fast.* Now that the twins were going to college, him and Emily could fuck whenever they wanted. Emily had her tubes tied so they could not have any more kids. Both of them agreed that they just wanted two, so Emily went to the doctor years ago after the twins started preschool. Emily and him fucked like there was no tomorrow. *I love that we can still have sex when we are 44 years old. Emily is the best thing that ever happened to me.*

Chapter 18

Emily and Elijah were now retired and living by themselves. Amelia and Louis had moved out a few months ago and had found their significant others. The twins had married their soul mates. Emily was crying at both of their weddings. She couldn't believe that her daughter and son were all grown up now. *I can still remember when they were babies and I held them in my arms for the first time in the hospital. Now they are in their 20's and married. I am so proud of them.* Emily looked at Elijah on the couch with a smile. He is such a wonderful person. *Elijah still makes me feel like an amazing woman.* She kissed him. He looked shocked afterwards. "What was that for?" Emily grinned and put her head on his chest, while holding his hand. "For being such an amazing man who always treats me right." He looks at her with so much passion in his eyes. "I love you Emily." She winked. "I love you too Elijah." They went up to the bedroom and fucked all night long.

Elijah and Emily started getting gray hair. They now had 3 grandkids, Amy, Simon and Scott. Emily loved singing to them and Elijah would play the guitar. He would glance at Emily out of the corner of his eye and think back to when they first started going out. Her hair was now filled with silver streaks and she still looked like the most beautiful woman in the world. *I am the luckiest man on earth to be with someone who is my equal in everything.* They still had sex just like when they were younger. Being with her made him feel like he was 18 years old again. After he played the guitar, Elijah held her close as they started to dance to a slow song. They saw Amelia and Louis roll their eyes. Their children knew that they were cheesy and corny. Elijah and Emily noticed that Amy, Simon and Scott were looking at them too. One day when their grandkids were older, they would tell them about their love story and pass it down to generations to come. He smiled at Emily. Elijah had such a great life with   her.   He   didn't   have   any   regrets.

Chapter 19

Emily grinned as Elijah was talking to Amy, Simon and Scott, their grandkids about their relationship. "I met your grandmother when we were 18 years old. I thought that she was the prettiest girl that I have ever seen. Now I think that she is the most beautiful woman in the universe." Amelia sighed. "Dad, did you have to wait to tell them when they are 18?'' Elijah grinned. "I figured that I would hold back on telling them the whole story until they were old enough to hear the adult parts. Plus it's only appropriate that I tell my grandkids, your mother and I's story when they are 18 because that's when we met." Louis was annoyed. "But you guys have told this story to us since we were 6." Emily winked. "Technically, we told you two the clean version, when you were 6. Then when you were adults, we told you the whole story." Elijah and Emily laughed. Amelia replied "you two are so corny." Elijah smiled. "But you love us Amelia and so does Louis." Louis sarcastically retorted "depending on the day dad." Elijah and Emily looked at Amelia and Louis talk to their spouses.

He put his arm around his wife Sara. "Sorry about my dad's corniness." Sara grinned at him. "I think your mom and dad are really cute. They are old but your dad tells the story like he is still young." Louis smiled. "Yeah, he does that. I love him and my mom though. They are still in love, which is crazy. I'm glad that they waited to tell Simon and Scott about the sex parts." Sara giggled. "I feel the same way, Louis. The way they tell the tale, it is very explicit." Louis laughed. "Yes, it is definitely racy. My parents are great though. Amelia and I had a good childhood." Sara replied, "That's good, Louis." They kissed.

Amelia looked at her husband Adam and shrugged her shoulders. "They have been like this since Louis and I were young." Adam grinned. "I think it's sweet that they still love each other after all these years. Them telling Amy after she is 18 makes sense. Their love story does get graphic for little kids anyway." Amelia and Adam laughed. She put her arms around Adam. "You are right. They are adorable. My parents are 75 years old and they still act like they are in their 20's. I hope that we can be like that." Adam winked. "I know that we are going to be like that. We are not that much older than them." Amelia sighed. "I know." Adam smiled. "Don't worry, Amelia. Amy is going to college soon and then it will be just the two of us. You know what that means?" He wagged his eyebrows. Amelia smacked him playfully. "We are not my parents, Adam." Adam laughed. " I know, but they are a good example." Amelia giggled. "If you think so." Adam dipped her and kissed her.

Emily and Elijah had smiles on their faces from seeing their son and daughter happy. Their grandkids were busy on their phones. Elijah yelled "you know there are more important things in life than being on your phones." Emily saw Amy, Simon and Scott roll their eyes in unison. Amy responded "we know that you guys are old now. You wouldn't understand." Elijah frowned. "Your grandmother and I may be old but we still find time to have fun." He came up to

Emily and started doing the tango with her. She grinned. Emily stared into Elijah's eyes. *Even in old age, he still makes my heart skip a beat.* Amy, Simon and Scott were not impressed, but they would understand once they found their soulmates.

Chapter 20

Elijah and Emily sat on their porch swing looking out at fields. Elijah looked at Emily. "Remember when we first met?" Emily laughed. "How could I forget? I stuttered and said that you were cute." Elijah smiled. "Yeah, you did say that. Do you want to know what I thought of you?" Emily shrugged. "Did you think I was some weird girl who came on too strong?" He shook his head. "No. I thought that you were adorable. You were so pretty and you are still beautiful even now." He saw Emily start to cry. "Elijah Robert Henderson, you always know just what to say to make me feel loved." Elijah smiled. "I only speak the truth, Emily. I love you as much as I did when we went on our first few dates. I missed you so much when we were apart. I was so miserable." Emily grinned. "I love you as much as I did back then too Elijah. I couldn't stop thinking about you when we were apart. I was depressed for months. I thought that I wouldn't be able to get out of bed. One day though, I started going out to society. I tried going out on dates but none of them were you. There is only one man who has ever held my heart and that is you." Elijah was so happy that she said that. "I am so glad that you were sad too. I also attempted to go out with girls, but I never felt that connection that I do with you. You have always occupied my heart, Emily Rose Henderson. I am so pleased that we have two kids, three grandkids and four great grandkids." Emily squeezed his hand just like the old days, and he went through their relationship in his head. They had their good times and their bad times. Him and Emily went through so many firsts together. First date, first date, first time they had sex, when they had the twins and having the grandkids and great grandkids. He taught Louis and Simon and Scott how to play the guitar when they were younger. Elijah would have shown his great grandsons Joshua and Harrison how to play, but by that time his fingers were starting to get arthritis. He loved his life with Emily and he would not change a single thing. *Who knew that bumping into Emily all those years ago would lead to them sitting here holding hands?* He kissed Emily.

Emily kissed Elijah back just like when they were 18. As they pulled apart, she thought back to when they first met and how shy she was. Emily has grown so much since then. She even remembered the dark times when her and Elijah weren't together and that period does not make her sad. Those two years that they were apart, helped both of them realize that they needed time to do their own things. She smiles now thinking about it because her and Elijah have done so much together since then. They had a daughter and a son, a granddaughter and two grandsons and two great grandsons and two great granddaughters. She was so proud of Amelia and Louis. They are all grown up now. Emily still thought back to when they were babies and she was changing their diapers. Amy, Simon and Scott were grown now too. Amy had Amanda and Addison, while Simon had Harrison and Scott had Joshua. Joshua, Harrison, Amanda and Addison were starting preschool next week. Time goes by so fast. She looked at Elijah and put her arm around him. "I'm so glad that I met you, Elijah." He smiled at her and held her in his arms. "I'm so happy that I met you too Emily. You are the best thing that has ever happened to me." Emily grinned. "You are the best thing that has ever happened to me too, Elijah." They sat there gazing at each other with so much love. *I am so thankful that I found my soulmate in high school. Elijah and I have had such a great life together. I would not have it any other way.*

The   End

Dedications

To Joshua, the love of my life. You have always inspired me and made me a better person. You push me out of my comfort zone and have made me into a strong, confident woman. You are my Elijah. This is for you.

To Kyle, my little brother who is basically my twin. You have always been there for me. You help me be a better writer. Thanks for helping edit this book. I couldn't have done it without you. I love you bro.

To Mom, who has always been my biggest supporter since I was born. When the doctors thought I couldn't do certain things because I am autistic, you never gave up hope. You have always been my biggest cheerleader, and for that I am grateful.

To Harry, my brother from another mother. You are so sweet and helpful. Thank you for also helping me edit this book and for supporting me.

To Scott, the comedic relief of the book. Thank you for your sense of humor and for always making me laugh. You embody Samuel every day of your life.

To Placeit.com for helping me make my own book cover.

To Nicholas Sparks for writing such great romance books and for inspiring me to write one.

To James Patterson for writing my favorite book Sunday's at Tiffany's.

To Olive Garden for always having great italian food to eat.

To All-Time Low for writing Remembering Sunday, a great beautiful song.

To Taylor Swift for writing great breakup songs and for writing Lover, a great beautiful album.

To anyone who reads this book or buys it, thank you for liking my romance book. Thank you for the support. I appreciate it.

www.ingramcontent.com/pod-product-compliance
Lightning Source LLC
Chambersburg PA
CBHW020542130626
46552CB00007B/2726